A special Better Bullying thank you to:

Pastor Matthew Gallashaw
and the Helping Hand Rescue Mission volunteers

And to the Kyle Korver Foundation

And to the dedicated staff at
Kearny Elementary in North Philadelphia

And to Angel's Mom, Johnnie Mae Williams.
And Angel's little brother Savion (a bullying inspiration)

To sponsor our work in Philadelphia, donations are
welcomed: "The Helping Hand Rescue Mission"
AB: PO Box 14057, Philadelphia, PA, 19122

Please do not use or recreate any part of this book without
written permission. You are not allowed to and we asked
nicely.

-----2015-----

Please visit us at:
www.betterbullying.com
kylekorverfoundation.com
helpinghandphilly.org

or email Mr. Adam and Angel at:
betterbullying@gmail.com

-----2015-----

Cover Design: Milton Fox
Poem Credit: Sean Peterson
Logo Credit: Joseph Perez
Logo Assist: Dahnejha Jones

"in everything, do to others what you would have
them do to you"(Matthew 7:12)

Better

BULLYING

Mr. Adam Bruckner
And Angel Williams

Chapter 1

My little brother's feet smell terrible. Like a funky wet armpit. And his socks are rust colored. He always takes his shoes off and puts his toes on my chair while we are eating breakfast. It makes me want to throw up in my mouth. Then he crunches his cereal like a lion eating a lizard. And sings into his spoon. He is the most annoying 4th grader in the galaxy. And he is always getting me in trouble.

I was just in the Principal's office today because of him. When he was in the school bathroom this afternoon, he got a wet willy, swirly, and a purple nurple. That didn't happen because his feet smell, that happened because he is not tough enough.

Range Line Elementary has a bullying problem and I am mad as an iron about it. I am not upset that my brother's head is getting **flushed** in the toilet. I am upset that the **flusher** might get kicked out of school. You see, I am not mad at my brother's bully. I am his bully. I'm just trying to fix him. And I am in big big trouble for it.

Now I have to prove to the school that what I am doing is for his own good. I have to show them that I am just helping to toughen him up. To make him a man. They say it is bullying. I call it Better Bullying, and I want to use it to save the school.

Chapter 2

When bullying is done for good, it's called 'Better Bullying.' It's not just for little brothers, it is for anyone who needs to be fixed. It's a powerful tool to motivate kids, raise money, and to toughen up wimps so that they can handle the pain of this ruthless world without crying like they still have an umbilical cord.

There are some bad bullies in the world, and part of Better Bullying is to take them down. Cyber bully cowards are the worst. And there are some that bully based on skin color. I can assure you that my formula for Better Bullying only focuses on 2 colors.....**black&blue.**

And I am sick of the wimpy kid glorification. We all know that only the strong survive. I don't understand why the school coddles the weaklings instead of trying to repair them. If the teachers won't do it, my group will.

And that is why we must fight to reject **BILL215.** Principal Deitz is pushing the district to accept a new school law called **BILL215. BILL215** would allow teachers to expel bullies and force them into home schooling. WITH. THEIR. MOTHERS!!!!! I would have to steal my own lunch money and punch myself in the face if that happened to me.

Principal Deitz's changes have gone too far. First he switched our school colors from red and black to teal. As a color, teal is like the weak decrepit puked up little brother of navy blue. Just looking at it makes me sad as a mime. Then he outlawed gym class dodge ball. And now he wants to declare Range Line a **'Bully Free'** school. That's unnecessary. I have been **bullying for free** for years.

Chapter 3

Even though my little brother is a poodle on a pit-bull playground, he is still really popular. He has a cute girlfriend, a lot of buddies, and he gets grades from the beginning of the alphabet.

Despite all of his good fortune, he is crying right now because I am looking at him and punching my fist into my palm. He will never win a fight, be able to survive harassment, or stand up for himself in this mean world if his eyes water at these small

5

things. It's my job to toughen him up and I am going to do it well.

I don't want to use his name, but it's Timmy, and he sounds like a vacuum under water when he is upset. He stands, whimpers, and looks at me as his eyes leak and little snot bubbles grow out of his nostrils. I have a lot of work to do with him. He is 9 years old, so I don't have much time.

Timmy needs to get tougher and stronger to survive at Range Line Elementary when I leave after next year. I'm doing what I can to help, but I get in a lot of trouble for helping so much. My mom tells me to be nicer to him, and to never punch him. And I just punched him.

I guess I am going to have to explain to her what happened. Fortunately, during math class last month, I made a list of punching explanations, and now I just need to pick one. It is good to plan ahead.

"Yes Mom, I did punch Timmy, but I did it because....."

1. The cat wouldn't scratch his arm for him
2. There was a bug on him
3. I was cracking my knuckles as part of a science experiment to see if that gives me arthritis
4. In my dream last night he told me to

5. In Ireland it is good luck to punch your brother
6. It's a magic trick
7. I am preparing him to endure greater pain later in life
8. Punching is a brother's way of hugging
9. I was training my defensive skills in case we ever get kidnapped by a strange oaky mustached man in a van with no back windows who takes us and puts us in the circus and makes us wear tight and colorful outfits while playing with lions
10. It is his half-birthday

Chapter 4

I should probably introduce myself. Hi. My name is Vector. Vector Angelous Hall. 7th grader. I'm about 12 years old. About. I like to be a mystery. I am a bully. I am my brother's bully.

You probably laughed when you read my name. People always laugh at me. If you are an old person, you probably thought to yourself, "What's your Vector Victor?" That's a joke from an old person's movie about airplanes called Airplane. Not very creative.

I am used to getting teased. It doesn't bother me at all. Seriously it doesn't. Really, believe me, it doesn't. I do wish I had a different name though. Something normal. My brother Timmy got a normal name.

I guess my dad named me Vector after a <u>Star Wars</u> novel that never became a movie. Vector Prime. Vector is also a security system, a Nigerian rock band, and something in Physics. I like that Vector is a security system. I am kind of a security system for Timmy.

Timmy has always been really popular. I haven't. It makes me mad as a mosquito on a Barbie doll that he gets so much attention. But attention isn't going to keep him safe. I am. And that is why I am committed to Better Bullying.

Chapter 5

My Mom thinks I am jealous of Timmy because he has a dad around. And a real girlfriend. And a lot of friends.

I may not have as many friends as Timmy, but I have a best friend. And Jam (his real name is Jamison) is not only a best friend, but he is a best bully friend. Jam's dad is the football coach at the high school and he has muscles like a cartoon. And Jam is on the Vicious Falcons, the first place 7th grade football team in Roseville County. Jam doesn't play much on the team. His dad says he has old fat knees. They play catch a lot. I never met my dad, but I heard a lot about him. I don't care. Really. Seriously.

Like me, Jam has a little brother that is always getting him in trouble. I thought it was funny when he put his brother in the dryer. It's not like he left it on the super spin cycle. And I think there is some charm with giving a little brother a bowl of yogurt that is actually mayonnaise, but Jam's mom didn't think so.

Chapter 6

Jam is like a brother to me, but he is not my brother. Timmy is my brother, but he isn't good for much other than doubling my allowance. He calls it stealing, and I call it sharing.

We share a room too. I am on the top bunk. I tell him the kidnappers will definitely take him first because it is easier to snatch the low kid. And I like to dangle fake spiders onto his face while he sleeps. These things toughen Timmy up.

Timmy's dad lives with us sometimes, but he travels a lot too. He drives a truck as big as a house around the country. He gets to honk that big seal horn and eat while he drives and says things like 'breaker breaker.' He is one of the old people that says, "What's your Vector Victor?" I like him because he is nice to me. And he has a special handshake for us, and he brings us magnets. He tells us to be the best we can be. That's how I know I need to be the best bully I can be.

I have never met my dad. I think I said that already.

Chapter 7

Mr. Blade has a big bald head. Like a pool ball with a nose, eyes, mouth, and ears. And he has a creepy forehead vein that comes out when he gets mad. It's as big as a garden hose, but you can only see it when he is upset. And he always wears thick cologne that smells like a mall. And he has arms bigger than some Kindergarteners. And he often wears a short sleeved shirt and a big fat tie. And he does not like me one small bit.

He is my English and Math teacher. And last week Mr. Blade said that our school has a bullying problem. He told us that there was a vote coming up by the school board and student council that would allow Principal Deitz to expel bullies. They named it **BILL215**. It would be a new school law. Mr. Blade asked us to use our computer time to look up some facts about bullying, to take notes, and then we had a class talk.

After 10 minutes, I was the first to raise my hand and said, "I used Google and found out that the word 'bully' actually used to mean 'sweetheart.' It was a good word when it was born. And then it changed. Maybe the word got bullied and it changed." Everyone laughed except for Mr. Blade. I love it when people laugh with me and not at me.

Chapter 8

Mr. Blade talked for about 10 more minutes, but I wasn't listening because I was thinking of another way to be funny. And counting the number of tiles on the wall. There are 358. They are small tiles. And there were 2 pencils stuck in the ceiling.

And then I was trying to figure out if the fan had 3 or 4 different arms spinning. I almost figured it out when Mr. Blade said, "Maybe Victor, I mean Vector wants to tell us more." The class laughed when he called me Victor. I hate it when he does that, and he does it a lot. One time he called me Hector. And another time he called me Vectory, like the word victory. I really hated that time, especially because kids laughed a lot.

So when he called me Victor and told me to share what I learned, I guess I forgot I was a kid or something. I really wanted people to laugh with me and not at me so I read from my computer notes like a robot in a deep flat voice. Like a robot, **"Bully. Is. An. Old. Word. From. About. 1530. That. Used. To. Mean. Sweetheart. And. I. Think. Bullies. Are. Good. Because. They. Teach. Kids. To. Fight. Back. And. Makes. Them. Tougher. And. The. Word. Is. Overused. And. Abused. And. Some. Bullies. Get. Paid. They. Are. Hockey. Players."**

I was a pretty good robot for a minute in my life. I never broke form. Still, I noticed something once I was done reading; it got real quiet. Quiet like a unicorn. Quiet like how it always gets when Mr. Blade gets done screaming, but he wasn't screaming. I think everyone thought he was about to, but he was just looking at me with his forehead vein about to burst. And he said, "I think Nector is going to do a little extra homework tonight. I have a book on bullying for him to read. Here you go **Nector**." I know a few kids laughed, but it was still really quiet.

He gave me this little book called, "The Truth About Bully Goats." And then the bell rang. I couldn't tell if I was in trouble. I was pretty sure I was in trouble. I took the book and put it in my bag and left quickly and quietly.

On the walk home I took the bullying book out of my bag and hit Timmy in the back of the head with it.

Chapter 9

I read the first 3 chapters of "The Truth About Bully Goats" before I even took my shoes off when I got home. I always take my shoes off so I don't get in trouble by getting mud on the floor. That one time the house looked like a footprint factory.

Like I was saying, I was so interested in the book that I just sat on the front steps and read. It was an adorable book. I think that the point was to say that the bully goat was like the bully in schools. And that bullies are usually not as big and as bad and as mean on the inside as they seem on the outside. Like I said, it was adorable.

Clearly bully goats aren't as tough as my friend Jam. He is as tough on the inside as the outside. One time an elder bully tried to take Jam's sandwich during lunch. It was in 4th grade, the year before he grew a mustache. Jam wanted the meat (roast beef) in the sandwich, so he pulled it out and put it in his lunch box. Then he put his hand between two pieces of potato bread and punched that kid in the nostril and asked him if he liked that sandwich. **That knuckle sandwich**. That was the day Jam became my hero.

Anyway, I read the rest of the bully goat book that night, before and after dinner. Dinner was macaroni and cheese with scrambled eggs and bacon mixed in. My mom can really cook like a tv show.

We had one scoop of mint brownie ice cream for dessert and I accidentally licked my finger and put it in the middle of Timmy's bowl. I accidentally do that a lot during desserts. And that made Timmy not want his, so I accidentally had 2 bowls of mint brownie ice cream.

Chapter 10

I woke up the next morning and thought of the things I was grateful for in my life. Mom said that was a good exercise. I thought about how I was thankful for the gravity of Jupiter that pulled asteroids away from crashing into Earth and obliterating me before I had my first girlfriend. And I took a moment to appreciate the honeybees and the work they do, because plain Cheerios taste like wet cardboard. And I was thankful for the billy goat. I love java candy and the billy goat discovered coffee beans. That's what the book said.

I gave that book back to Mr. Blade when I strolled into class and said, "This was adorable, billy goats have rectangular pupils," and walked to my desk to sit down.

I forgot about the billy goat and his square eyes until ten minutes later when Mr. Blade asked me in front of the class, "Hector, would you like to tell us about the book you read?"

I didn't want to say 'adorable.' I knew that was a little rich. And I can't remember how it happened, but I had a super power for a minute and I stood up instead and said, "Deeee-licious." And then I sat down as the kids in class laughed. They really laughed like I was famous and popular. People always laugh when famous and popular kids say things, even when they do not get the jokes. And Mr. Blade did not get the joke. Or maybe he did and that was why he turned red as salsa.

He said, "Apparently Lector Hector Mector Vector thinks being a bully is funny. And he is going to have to write a paper on it and read it to the class. And if he doesn't, he certainly won't think it's funny when he gets his grade."

And as many know, I did write that paper. I really really did.

Chapter 11

The paper that I wrote that night was glorious. I think if I had asked any person in the hemisphere, they would have told me not to hand it in. That was why I didn't ask anyone. I wanted to hand it in. I wanted to have my moment. I wanted to shine. I wanted attention. I really wanted to make kids laugh. I wanted Shannon Ungerman to notice me and to like me. I wanted to be popular.

Shannon Ungerman was historically cute and as popular as MTV. She had hair like a shampoo commercial and always matched and sometimes wore polka dots.

And I really wanted her to like me. But she was often a little mean to me. I heard that sometimes girls are mean to the boys they like. And I thought that maybe she liked me a lot, because the only time I talked to her she opened her eyes as wide as a sunrise and didn't say anything. She just walked away.

In case she didn't like me, I needed something big to get her attention. And so that next day when I strutted into Mr. Blade's class, I made sure to pretend like I had forgotten about that paper I was supposed to write. I pretended like I had forgotten a lot of things. I didn't even bring a book bag or a pencil. I thought that was pretty cool.

And then just like I imagined, Mr. Blade asked me about it. It was right after the bell rang. I had lost sleep thinking about that great moment, and it was unfolding just as I had hoped. Mr. Blade said, "V-ExTore, do you have a paper to share with the class?"

I sure did. I took some toilet paper out of my pocket and blew my nose. Twice. I was really trying and said, "Sure. Anyone want to share my paper?" I tried not to look at Shannon Ungerman but I did.

And everyone laughed. Even me. Even Shannon Ungerman. I think the kids that were home sick from school probably even started laughing and didn't know why. It was a great moment in the history of 7th grade. And then I blew my nose on it again. Twice. And held it up.

Mr. Blade said, "Well I think that/" and then Emmie Jane got up and took the toilet paper from me and blew her nose into it. It was amazing. And gross. And everyone laughed so hard that they almost had to go to the hospital. It was unplanned but it was pure magic.

And then Mr. Blade went to war with the words coming out of his face.

Chapter 12

I cannot remember what happened exactly, but it was lawnmower loud. Mr. Blade pretended that he was a volcano with a tornado inside. Words spun and erupted and I think that he spit on Mia Rienzi in the second row. I wanted to say, "Say it don't spray it," but it was too late.

I knew I shouldn't push back any more. And that I should have just taken my lumps. You have to know that I couldn't stay silent. This was my moment. This was my destiny. So when he said, "Vector didn't bring anything to class except classlessness.

He thinks that he is perfect and can pick on others. Well, a news flash class. He holds his writing pencil like he is picking up a baby rabbit and trying not to hurt it. And his New Year's Resolution was to get waves in his hair. And he wants to be a comedian, and I hope you don't need to graduate from the 7th grade to do that kind of work, because he gets a failing grade for not writing the paper on bullying."

That was the moment where the sun shined upon my life. I had to decide to be forgotten or to be remembered. I had to make a decision between goodness and greatness. And I chose greatness. And I roared, **"I didn't forget anything!!!"**

Mr. Blade cut back, "Well you didn't bring a book bag, and the paper is due right now. And you can't go to your locker. So you fail."

I looked my life in the eyes and my words crashed out, **"I have it with me!!!"**

Every kid in the class turned to look at me. I am pretty sure that the other classrooms could see me through the walls. And I think angels probably gathered and floated by the ceiling. It was my moment. And it was so quiet.

Mr. Blade's big bald head turned red as blood and the vein sprouted like a garden snake on his forehead and he spoke 2 words, "GET IT!!!"

I don't know if Mr. Blade would have said that if he had known where I had kept the paper on bullying. It was in the back part of my underwear.

Chapter 13

I have been told about 350 times what I now know. I should have hid my paper in my socks. I didn't. I put it in my underwear. I don't know why. I guess I wanted people to laugh. I guess I wanted to be shocking. I guess I wanted Shannon to think I was as crazy as Jam and kiss me under the slide at recess. I guess I wanted to be famous. And I guess, I wanted to be in trouble.

I pulled my paper out of the top back of my pants and the class gasped. I think they all gasped at once like it was an opera or something. I actually don't know if people gasp at operas, but if they do, they sound like a 7th grade class when a bully yanks a Ziploc bag with a bullying paper in it out of his undies. They gasped.

And I can't remember if Mr. Blade asked me to read it or not, but I read it. I walked to the front of the room and I read it. Mr. Blade had been calling me all sorts of different names. And he had challenged me in front of the class, and I answered. I answered big time.

"Mr. Blade said he wanted to know if I would think bullying was funny once I had to write a paper on it. Let's see if you think it is funny.

Why did the bully cross the road?"

I really heard a cricket I think. No one said anything. I was off to a bad start, **"Why DID the bully cross the road?"**

Diego Johnson was a brave man, "To beat up the chicken?"

People laughed cautiously. I was a little jealous so I cut in early on the laughs, "TO GET TO THE OTHER FIGHT!!!"

I think someone clapped. I can't remember. It doesn't matter because I kept going, "Knock knock?"

"Who is there?" Sydney Leplae sang like an angel from the front row.

"Bully"

"Bully **WHOOO**?" Wesley Goodman asked in his best owl voice.

"Bully Jean is not my lover," I sang the words of the Michael Jackson song. I don't know if anyone got it. I learned it that morning on YouTube. I didn't care. I just kept going, "So I saw 5 bullies beating up a

Kindergartener today. I was going to stop the fight, but I didn't know who started it. And on the way to school today I saw a homeless guy with a sign that said, 'NEED CHANGE FOR A HAMBURGER' and he had a cup. I thought it was early for such a big meal, but I said, '*Thank you I do need change for a hamburger*' and I took his cup full of money and went to McDonald's. My brother saw me take the money and said I was a bully. I said he looked like an elf. He said, '*sticks and stones may break my bones but words will never hurt me.*' So I picked up a rock and broke his nose with it. And why did the bully **kick** the/"

I didn't finish my next joke when Mr. Blade yanked my shirt collar like he was pulling a cord to start a lawnmower. Mr. Blade snatched me and was dragging me to the door. I really tried to get in one last joke on my way out. It was hard for Mr. Blade to turn the knob with me in his grip so I got an extra second. On the way out I yelled, "Why did the bully **kick** the computer?"

I was out the door as I answered, "He was supposed to **boot** up the system."

Chapter 14

I really hoped that Shannon had laughed. I was afraid to look at her during my speech. I hoped she had seen that I was brave. And that people noticed me. And that I mattered. And I hoped that I was finally popular.

I didn't know what was going to happen with my popularity, but I knew I was in trouble. Mr. Blade dropped me off, said something to the secretary, and I had to sit in the room outside of Principal Deitz's office. That was where the secretary had her desk and where the kids came to wait for the nurse after they threw up Fruit Loops and French toast.

There were 5 chairs and I was sitting in the corner one, and there was a girl in the middle seat. I barely noticed her, but she looked sad. I just rested my forehead on my hand and my elbow on my right knee. I was trying to sleep. I didn't sleep much the night before because I was so excited to be popular.

The next thing I know, the secretary Miss McCurdy, woke me with a mean bark, "Where are you Vector?"

I wasn't confused and I didn't think she was, but I said, "Mentally or physically?"

She was looking right at me, so I think we both knew what she meant and it was not good. She was mad as a hornet. I mean, she was really ticked off at me. She made some *tisking* sounds and said something about **BILL215** and talked to herself and shook her head like she was trying to get water out of her ears.

I realized something in that moment. I wasn't just in trouble. I was trouble.

Chapter 15

I heard the girl in the middle seat make a noise like a sprinkler and I looked at her. She was crying. She was crying real tears. She had teddy bear brown hair and her arms were crossed over her stomach like she was sick. "Are you sick?" I asked.

She looked at me with sad eyes. They had red marks like wrong answers on a test. I didn't know her name, but I had seen her around the school. Her words were careful like a scared cat looking in an empty room for a dog, "No, I'm not sick."

I didn't even think about not saying something, "Why are you crying?"

She didn't look at me this time, "Because I am fat." I could only see her right eye from where I was sitting, but she didn't blink. It was like she was reading the words off the floor.

I looked at her stomach to check, but her arms were guarding my view. I didn't think she was fat. She wasn't fat. I didn't know why she was crying because she wasn't fat. "You are not fat."

"Josh Crans said I was 'a fat cow.'" Her face and shoulders deflated, giving up hope.

I didn't understand. She wasn't fat. I wanted to see, "Stand up."

This time she looked at me and her eyes opened like umbrellas. I realized I had said a very dumb thing. I say dumb things sometimes, but I also make amazing saves sometimes. "**Stand up** and walk over to Josh Crans and rip his heart out with a spoon. You are not fat. You are normal sized. You are perfect. Why did he say that?"

She wheezed, "Josh Crans said that all girls look like animals. Either like cats or birds. I asked him which one I was and he said, '*Neither. You are either a dog or a cow. A fat cow.*' Josh Crans is a bully!!!" Her face became a wet strawberry, "Why are you here?"

Before I could say anything, that secretary Miss McCurdy cut in, speaking over her stapler, "**For being a bullyyyyyy.**"

And the crying girl shot me a look that showed I was the one who just had his heart ripped out with a spoon.

Chapter 16

After Kelly was done stabbing me with her eyes, I explained what had happened in class. I had to whisper like a dolphin to her because the curmudgeonly secretary was mostly unimpressed with the last few things I had to say. And then an interesting thing happened. Kelly stopped crying and started laughing. She thought my story was hilarious. She was squirting laughs out of her cheeks when I told her about the toilet paper. She really laughed like her face was popping bubbles. And it kind of made me *like* her a little. Not '*like like*,' but I did kinda *like* her a little.

Kelly finally took her hands away from her stomach while she was laughing and I looked to see if she was fat. She wasn't fat. I didn't care if she was, but I kind of wanted to know. She said, "You are funny Vector." And those words were like a hungry breakfast to me. It felt really important to hear.

I felt like I should say something and said, "And I don't even know your name, but you are not fat or ugly. You are not skinny like a deer, but I don't think girls should be skinny like a deer. I think you got it just right. And just remember, hurt people hurt people. Someone probably hurt Josh Crans. And I think he has a fat head. Or just a big fat forehead. It's like a 5head."

She laughed so hard she blew a snot rocket on her knee. That's a true story. I saw it and she saw it. That really happened. And then she said, "I'm Kelly Chrisinger. And I don't want to be mean towards mean people. Then it makes us the same. Thank you though. You made me feel better. Let's not say mean things about Josh."

I agreed not to say anything mean about Josh. He deserved much worse than that. Josh Crans had broken the rules of bullying. And he was going to pay for it.

Chapter 17

Word spread like spilled lunch tray milk about my bullying jokes and my detentions. It was remarkable. Incredible. My plan had worked. Kids were talking about me. I was popular. I wasn't just a bully. I was the bully. And I wasn't alone.

When I walked into the lunchroom, 7th grade bullies surrounded me like garbage can

27

bees. I didn't even have to ask, I just knew that they were in the club and came to me to show support. Three fist bumps, a high five, and 2 chest pounds later, and I knew every bully in 7th grade was standing with me.

I wasn't elected, I was selected. I was the Bully King. There were 7 of us, and I knew from watching leadership infomercials that I had to seize the moment and be a leader. So I called a secret bully meeting after school. I told the other guys to meet me in the woods by the dead tree near the netless soccer goal at 3:17pm. I told them we would not meet for longer than 15 minutes. I told them we were going to mobilize our forces and unite. I told them it was time for Better Bullying. And then I walked by Josh Crans and accidentally knocked his food tray out of his hand. And his chocolate milk spilled everywhere.

Chapter 18
3:17pm

The earth was damp beneath our secret meeting spot. It was the kind of place that never got enough sun and permanently smelled like road kill intestines. It was slimy and gross. It was perfect.

The selected 6 looked towards me to lead. No one joked. No one spoke. The soggy earth was mine. This was my pack to lead. It was my moment.

And as I opened my mouth to begin the new chapter of life for Range Line Elementary's Bullying Legion, my words got stuck like a winter coat zipper chewing fabric. I stuttered. I stammered. I stumbled.

I looked at these chosen boys as they looked to me. There was no one to save me. No turning back. I had to stare my future in the face and choose which life I wanted to live. And I chose greatness!!! In a moment that did not exist within my bowels on the day before, I spoke life, "Young men, I know you are listening, but I need you hear me." I knew I misspoke but I sounded like a pirate so I kept going, "The silence of a thousand bullies screams from the past. I am sick and tired of being sick and tired. There are posters and posers at this school that are talking about the same things: STOP BULLYING NOW. There is even **BILL215** that would allow Principal Deitz to expel bullies from the school.

"This is a new day. A movement. We are going to be like a bad armpit rash that keeps coming back."

My words flowed like syrup, "There are 2 kinds of bullies in this world. Those who think that they can and those who think that they can't and they are both right. Which are you? You are the chosen ones. Will you accept this choosing? Will you join with me in Better Bullying?"

Jam, from the football team, was always intense and said, "The gallon of blood in my body pumps for the cause!!!"

Mick, shaped like a soda can, who believed in equality for all said, "For their own good, I will bully brown, white, and yellow kids until they are bloody red."

Dante, who wanted to end global poverty said, "Bully it from the rich, give it to the poor."

Carl, the heavy weight wrestler son of a Pastor, proclaimed, "As sure as God made green apples my word is yes."

Serg, who had a Marine brother, and only spoke in 2 word clips declared, "AFFIRMATIVE VECTOR."

Glenn, who was smart as a book, said, "I am because WE will be, and since we now are, therefore I am."

Carl looked at him with confused skinny eyes and said, "Your what hurts?"

Glenn smiled and said, "I am with you. I am in for Better Bullying."

Chapter 19

We met again in 3 days. I was super excited. I wanted us to be emotionally healthy bullies. Open communication. We agreed to have identical voting power in the movement, but they said I was the first among equals. It was humbling.

I said that where we would go one, we would go all. I told them I knew that if I built it, they would come. And I knew that it was time for every bully to protect a weak kid and say, 'show me the money.' Basically I was out of things to say and just started quoting movies.

I had a vision to make Range Line a safer and healthier place. And I had a team. Better Bullying was going to do great things. We bullied for good. We were organized and orderly.   We had structure. And we worked together.

We shared ideas about how to hunt and gather soft children who were always escaping.

Serg said his two words, "They run."

Glenn was always quoting dead people and added, "In running it is man against himself, the cruelest of opponents."

Carl preached, "Then we shall call them **RUNNERS**." And that was how we decided to change Range Line, by catching the **RUNNERS**.　And fixing those wimps one by one.

Chapter 20

I shared my vision of toughening up the school weaklings to prepare them for this barbaric world.　And righting the many wrongs done by bad bullies.　And then I listened.

Jam said childhood obesity and diabetes had soared at Range Line.　And he was going to knock the sugar out of the chunky **RUNNERS**.　He smiled and said, "Plus, it hurts less to punch a porky kid."　He added, "We'll get their buns ready for Varsity football with my pappy."

Carl, whose dad is a Pastor, said kids needed to get back to church.　Since prayer was banned in school in 1962, Carl believed we had morally decayed as preteens.　And he was ready to do whatever it took to get kids into Heaven.　Even if he had to body slam them and drag them up the stairway.

Serg only said 2 words at a time. And that day it was, "American proud."　He wanted kids to only use products made in the USA.　And he hated when they wore Brazilian soccer hats or shirts written in a different language.　He would hunt down anyone in foreign fabric, but he would leave kids alone if they were patriotic.

Glenn vowed to beat students who got bad grades. He knew if they failed they wouldn't pay taxes as adults. He said he didn't want a school of lummox. Lummox is a fancy word for 'fool'. Glenn liked fancy words. And taxes. And fashion. Glenn hated when kids didn't match.

Dante wanted to help end world hunger by stealing **RUNNER'S** lunch money. For a dollar a day, he could feed a starving child in Africa. And he might just take your shoes and send them there too.

Mick despised inequality. He said he wanted to make sure we harassed, stole, and beat children of all ethnicities.

We were a great team. We had a compassionate, spiritual, nutritional, and social balance. That was Better Bullying.

Chapter 21

We agreed on the Better Bullying Bylaws (BBB) for **RUNNERS** and wrote down our core values. It was a working copy, but I was pretty proud of us.
1. No bullying girls
2. No bullying handicapped or disabled kids
3. No bullying children of veterans

4. No bullying with weapons
5. Bullying money goes to charity
6. Never break bones (yours or theirs)
7. Never bully a ninja
8. Bullying stops when the crying starts
9. No bully should hit a kid wearing glasses, unless they are stolen movie theatre 3D glasses or unless they are hipster glasses that are worn without the lenses just to look trendy
10. It is the bully's birthright to bully any red headed **RUNNER**, regardless of previously mentioned restrictions
11. No bragging or confessing
**Bullies accept credit cards, paypal, Venmo
***Our bullies are all certified in CPR.
(Please don't force us to demonstrate).

Chapter 22

Time was not wasted. In the hallway, I heard Rudy Will, a bad bully, teasing a boy about his stutter. Serg was with me when I kicked Rudy in the Patellar tendon of his right knee. Rudy fell to the ground crying like a wolf. Serg took bubble gum from the stutterer and mashed it into Rudy's hair. He chewed another piece and forced it into Rudy's mouth and said, 2 words, "Bullying stops." And then he took Rudy's Yankees hat, saw that it was made in China, and ripped the brim off with his teeth.

At the same time, Carl grabbed Shawn Seip by the nose and pinched til 3 blackhead zits popped. That boy hadn't been to church in 2 months. He promised to be back that Sunday, and Carl let go.

Down the hall, Glenn went through Tyler Lessard's backpack and saw that he had two D's and an F on his report card. He said, "It is impossible for a man to learn what he thinks he already knows."

Tyler said, "What?"

And Glenn said, "Exactly." And then he punched him in the ear and said, "Next time you get below a C, you will see my fist hit your favorite tooth."

In the bathroom Dante was charging people a buck for 5 squares of toilet paper. He collected $16 to send to Africa.

Jam was in the cafeteria making sure it was a healthy lunch. He spilled 17 sodas, knocked down 10 plates of fried chicken, and smashed 14 Twinkies.

And Mick saw James Dobbins bad bullying a minority 5th grader at recess. James Dobbins had stolen his favorite orange baseball. Mick snapped. He made an NFL tackle, and grabbed James Dobbins by the back of his underpants. Mick lifted him up off the ground and pulled until the waistband ripped. He didn't stop there. He couldn't. He pulled that underwear band all the way up, and wrapped it around James Dobbins's head. An underwear headband.

It was a great day. It was just the beginning. Better Bullying over bad bullying.

Chapter 23

Our bullying legend rose like high tide through the halls of Range Line Elementary. We kicked and tripped and disciplined at a feverish rate. We changed lives.

We were nearly famous, but we needed a signature statement. I told the Bully7 that we would never get a 3rd chance to make a 2nd impression. And like a good leader, I asked for ideas.

Serg said 2 more words, "Fear. Power."

Wow. That was deep for days. We needed to scare everyone so that they would follow us. Serg grabbed a #2 pencil with teeth marks and a skeleton of a pink eraser. He didn't speak, but he used his ancestral military training to map out the hallways.

Serg balanced our strengths and weaknesses. And mapped the perfect spot for our first attack. The stairwell near the English classrooms. **RUNNERS** couldn't run.

Between classes, the stairwell was thick with **RUNNERS**. Between 4th and 5th period, every pre-teen in the school climbed up and down those 20 stairs. There was no place to hide. And no place to run. And since students were coming from English class, they were carrying their largest paper load of the day and hadn't yet spent their lunch money.

Chapter 24

This was not a crude operation. It was with military precision at 11:14am, with the 7 of us staggered at different points of the stairwell, that we let it rain. Paper. It rained paper.

It was synchronized to happen at the same beautiful moment. Serg targeted a **RUNNER** named JC Cruz in a non-USA "Pura Vida" tshirt. He knocked the swollen homework folders out of his hand at the top of the stairs. Wow. Paper kick. Glenn was at the mid point and unzipped a **RUNNER's** very uncool Papa Smurf book bag. It was so full it looked like a white head zit exploded. Papers everywhere. Mick grabbed 2 **RUNNERS** who were often mean to girls, and banged their noses together. They both fell and clogged the stairs. Jam knocked a bag of sugary Skittles out of Henry Payne's hand on the first landing and empty calories skipped dangerously down. Dante punched a boy in $200 sneakers who had who refused to buy or use toilet paper that day during the Africa fundraiser. Gross. That **RUNNER** fell into the legs of the two 6th graders behind him. Those 2 were studying for a vocabulary test and dropped 200 index cards, which Jam accidentally kicked down the stairs. Carl dropped a gallon sized Ziploc filled with his dog's poop, Limburger cheese ravioli, and 5 sticks of melted butter. He didn't just drop it, he dropped it onto a kid who was using his cell phone in church the prior Sunday. This all happened at the same time that someone lit a smoking stink bomb at the top of the stairs.

Chaos erupted. Boys slipped. Girls screamed. Paper flew in the air. Pre-teens cried for help. Kids who were going up wanted to run down. Kids who were going down tried to run up. Panic. Terror. Hysteria. Claustrophobia. A new kid yelled for his mom. The stench crawled to our chins and we covered our noses for relief. The butter spread and the kids fell together in a tangled pile of knees and elbows and dog poop.

There were uncountable uncontrollable things happening on that staircase, but running was not one of them. We had attacked the one strength that they had, and the **RUNNERS** could not run.

Jam, Dante, and I stood blocking the bottom of the stairs. Serg, Glenn, and Carl barricaded the top. Kids were freaking out and flopping on the ground. They were trapped.

One by one, we let kids run out.....for a donation. We weren't stealing. They were begging us to take their money to help them escape that stench.

In 5 minutes we collected 3 pop tarts, an IOU for a German Shepard name Martini, and $97 in donations. It wasn't about the money, it was about the message. From that point forward, kids knew we were capable of keeping them clean in a mess, or making them the mess.

Chapter 25

The stairwell session was a success. Our dominant message got to everyone like a fart in an elevator. **There were new bullies at Range Line.** It was an amazing feeling to be proud of. It was a perfect execution except for one moment. Tommy Lunsford clawed his way up the stairs out of the pack by walking on students who were sprawled on their faces. He stepped on ribs and face cheeks and butt cheeks. He left a shoe print on Xavier Baur's shoulder blade. And he didn't pay a penny. He wasn't scared of us. He pushed Glenn to get through our barricade. Tommy Lunsford was a bad bully, and he was strong. He was a threat. And we needed to take him down.

Chapter 26

Our names were trending the next few days at Range Line Elementary. We were feared and respected. We were popular in our own way. And we were bullying brothers. I belonged. We belonged. It was the greatest week of my life.

It was not the greatest week of Principal Deitz's life. Parents complained about poop stained jeans, teachers called for emergency safety meetings, and he couldn't get any student to officially tell him what happened in the stairwell. That might have had something to do with a little advertising plan that Mick came up with called, "snitches get stitches."

We couldn't exactly tweet that out, so we whispered. A lot. We quietly said, "snitches get stitches" over and over as we walked the halls, sat on the school toilet in the middle stall, and on the bus. It spread. And no one said a word....but everyone knew. Even Principal Deitz knew.

Chapter 27

After our stairway slip show, a lot changed and a lot stayed the same. The economy of Better Bullying was excellent. **RUNNERS** gave us their lunch money as donations in exchange for protecting them from bullies in the school. And the **RUNNERS** needed protection. Especially from us. For a few dollars a day, their noses didn't get punched, their books didn't jump out of their hands on the stairwell, and they didn't accidentally get a wet willy.

For me, I was on top of a very small world. I was important. I was getting Shannon Ungerman to smile at me when I made jokes in Mr. Blade's class. I was talked about. I was respected. I was building a water well. I was in a great group of friends. I was popular.

I wasn't a good student. I wasn't nice to my little brother. I wasn't sleeping well at night. I wasn't invisible to dirty looks from teachers. And I wasn't forgotten by Mr. Deitz.

Mr. Deitz called me into his office for a special meeting that next week. I sat across from his desk, and nothing was said, but he was speaking to me with his eyes. And his cheeks kept twitching like he had a goldfish in his mouth. I could tell he had something to say, and he finally did when he handed me a medical journal or some psychology book that weighed a brick said, "Bully."

I said, "Rhymes with pulley." And I handed him back the book. I wish I had been funnier. That wasn't very funny at all.

At that point, the goldfish really started swimming in his mouth until he said, **"Look it up!!!"** and handed me back the book.

I didn't know why, but I kind of liked being bad and getting reactions from this man. I guess maybe I enjoyed the power of being in control because for so many years without my dad, I had no control. I don't know. I didn't care. I just opened up the book and turned to page 1. Then page 2. Then page 3. Then page 4. Then page 5.

Mr. Deitz released a noise like a dog makes when it gets stepped on in the dark. It wasn't the sound of a goldfish being bit. It wasn't human. It was a, "BRGGENNETCH NADIDASBSCHHHHESZZING" and then real words jumped out, "ALPHABETICALLY!!! **IT STARTS WITH BEEEEEEEE!!!!!!!**" He yelled like a tuba from his belly. I loved this.

I said, "Ohhhh." And then I turned to page 6. Then page 7. Then page 8. Then page 9.

Mr. Deitz ripped the book out of my hand like he was pulling a Band-Aid off my forearm. This time he spoke through his teeth without opening his mouth, **"OUT!!!!!"** as he pointed to the door.

I thought it was all pretty funny until I walked by crabby Miss McCurdy's secretary desk and Mr. Deitz barked to her, "Sally, get me the paperwork for **BILL215**."

Those goldfish were gone. I heard that loudly and clear. **BILL215** was the motion that would allow principals to expel bullies. This was bad. All bad.

Chapter 28

BILL215 was a big deal. A very big deal. There was a special committee made up of 2 school board members and Mr. Deitz.

That group was going to vote on **BILL215** after an open microphone debate in 2 Thursday nights. If the majority voted for the bill (2 out of 3), principals would be able to expel bullies for one year. If I was labeled a bully, I would be cast into the darkness of homeschooling with my mom. And I am positive that I would end up starting a band over a webcast with other homeschooled kids where we would make armpit fart noises with our cupped hands and laugh while studying Geometry and Constitutional History and I didn't want to be in an armpit farting band. I wanted to change Range Line Elementary School. I wanted to lead the movement of Better Bullying.

  BILL215 was not good for me. This was a problem. But I had other problems. Two other problems to be exact. Josh Crans and Tommy Lunsford. The bad bullies of Range Line Elementary.

Chapter 29
  The Bully7 is what I called our group of 7 bullies. I thought of that name because we were bullies and there were 7 of us. And it was easy to remember for Jam. Jam isn't

the sharpest spoon in the drawer. That's what his dad says about him.

Anyway, the Bully7 decided that we needed to build up our character defense before the vote on **BILL215**. That's how we decided to volunteer at the nursing home called Alexian Village. We thought it would be important to tell the voting committee that we were good guys. And we thought it would be nice to help some old people before they died.

Not all of the old people drooled, but some did. And not all were in wheelchairs but some of them were. Some of them seemed like they were frozen, and some were just normal people, but really old. They all smelled antique, usually like mothballs or mouthwash.

We went there a few Saturdays in a row and played checkers and chess and Connect4 and Go-Fish. Carl said we should let them win, but we decided that was soft, and that they wouldn't want anyone handing them tainted victories before they died. It was great fun, but the most important thing that happened was that we met this guy named Joey. He was in high school, but I am pretty sure he wouldn't have gotten an A in any of my 7th grade classes.

He thought that the 9-11 tragedy was named after 911 phone calls. And he has a twin sister, and still believes his mom was pregnant for 18 months with them. And another time when I told him I was learning about Rosa Parks in school, he thought that was a basketball court. When I corrected him, he asked me how many states there were and walked away and yelled, "**FIFTY!!!!**" before I answered.

Chapter 30

Joey cut old people's toenails for as long as they were at Alexian Village before they died. It was kind of gross, but he said if he didn't do it, no one would. And it was hard for them to ask. Especially if they were frozen.

Joey was a volunteer there too. He shaved the hair off of his arms and could make his muscles dance like piano keys. He was a bit of a hero to us.

We told Joey about **BILL215** and our bullying problem, and he introduced us to his friends Phoenix and Nate. They were much smarter than Joey. I am not supposed to tell anyone about what they told us, but after we met with them, we had some ideas about how to get the voting committee to agree with us. And I learned how to break into that bad bully Tommy Lunsford's email and ruin his life.   And we discovered how to make sure Josh Crans would never call a girl fat again, especially when she wasn't fat. But that was a different story.

Chapter 31

Having pizza with Joey, Phoenix, and Nate was hilarious.   They were high school funny. They kept saying Joey was Jam's dad, but I am almost positive that they were kidding. Joey was only 17 or 18. They were definitely just kidding.

They told us many stories that I can't repeat. One of those was about their friend Bobby who has gone away forever. He used to run a thing called the "Justice League." He stopped bad bullies in his own way, but I can't tell anyone about it. It is a crazy story. Someone wrote an article about him called, "This White Boy," but I never read it.

They offered to help us to honor their friend Bobby. They taught us a lot. I can't tell you what else they said, but after we met with them, we decided to mangle Josh Crans and Tommy Lunsford, and we knew how to do it. And we did it.

Josh Crans was a bad bully. No plan. No purpose. No progress. He was just mean and mad. And we made sure he knew about Better Bullying. Or maybe we didn't do anything to him. I am not supposed to say.

Chapter 32

Tommy Lunsford. Tommy Lunsford looked like he had been built by a Russian computer. He was stronger, faster, and quicker than any of us. He was a wrestler, and his ears looked like they had melted at the top. Cauliflower ear or something.

Maybe we got to him and maybe we didn't. If we did anything to him, it was hacking into his email, Facebook, and iCloud account. And then maybe we found selfies of him in his mom's dress and lipstick. And his online diary. And his list of girls that he rated in order. And who he thought was cute.

And maybe we knew how to send him an anonymous untraceable email threatening to release all of his personal information. And maybe he begged us not to. And maybe he stopped bullying people. Maybe he became ordinary. This all might have happened, but Joey and Nate and Phoenix taught us to keep our mouths shut. Or at least they might have.

If that all did happen, the Bully7 would have sworn to secrecy. To never confess if questioned. To never rat. To never talk to anyone outside of the Bully7 about it. Or even to speak to each other about it unless we were in a secure location. None of the junk we had on Tommy Lunsford was ever supposed to be released if he complied. And as better bullies, we would have promised to never break our oath to Tommy Lunsford or to each other.

And that is why what happened was so crazy!!!!!

Chapter 33

Tommy Lunsford wasn't the only bad bully in 8th grade. Josh Crans. Josh Crans was like gum on the bottom of my shoe that I couldn't get rid of. He had called Kelly a cow once, but he was also just a terrible little shower of mean words at Range Line. He wasn't big or strong, he was just ruthless.

He was a lawnmower in a garden. Mean names. Sarcastic fame. And everyone else was to blame. He was as useless as a dried up rubber band. A bad bully. He needed to be stopped.

We couldn't figure out the password to his online accounts, so we did some old school smash mouth terrible stuff. Or at least we heard that somebody did. Maybe I don't know who it was that got to him in the bathroom.

Someone or some group of 7 grabbed him when he was alone one day by the urinal. They roughed him to the bones. Scary stuff. A bloody nose and chipped tooth told the story even when no one else did.

It doesn't matter what happened that day, but something did. And Josh Crans stopped saying mean things. He was afraid to. And his bad bullying ended. And I heard he even apologized to Kelly.

I heard that this all happened one week before **BILL215** was voted on. That's what I heard.

Chapter 34

Things were different at Range Line during those weeks. I was confident and people knew who I was and they respected me. I was popular. Or at least I think I was popular. I am pretty sure I was popular. And no one rejected me. I hate rejection.

My little brother Timmy was getting a little bit tougher. He didn't cry when I looked at him. Only when I punched him or twisted his nipple. That's a purple nurple. And the more popular I got, the less I wanted to bully him. That was weird. I still took his lunch money, but I wasn't as jealous of his girlfriend, especially with Shannon Ungerman laughing at all of my jokes in class.

Shannon Ungerman was really starting to pay attention to me. And good attention this time. She called me over to her locker one day after school and I slid towards her like a magnet. She asked me for help with the math quiz. I asked her if she wanted to study, but she had a better idea. She knew that Mr. Blade kept the answer key in his desk. She wondered if I wanted to share it with her and get good grades. I felt like I was in the front seat of a rollercoaster. There was a rush of emotion when she asked me. Electricity. Included. In. Popular. I asked, "You are going to share the answers with me?"

She closed her locker and looked at me with both of her eyes into both of my eyes and said, "If you sneak into the room after school and copy down the answers, you can share it with me." And then she walked away like a movie star.

Chapter 35

During gym class on Friday, I asked to use the bathroom and instead ran up to the class. Mr. Blade wasn't in the room, so I sleuthed to his desk and opened the top drawer, using my shirt sleeve so I didn't leave fingerprints or DNA. Shannon Ungerman was right. All of the answer keys were in the drawer.

I didn't take the test. It was too risky. And I didn't know if I wanted to. I had never cheated before. But I had also never been popular before. And I had never had a girlfriend before. And Shannon Ungerman was my dream girl. And if I got that test, she was gonna go out with me. I think.

She was really popular and really really pretty, and had skin without zits. No blackheads or whiteheads and she wasn't a red head. Just skin. She was really really pretty, but she wasn't really really that nice. She definitely wasn't as nice as Kelly. Kelly was as nice as a kitten without claws. She smiled at everyone and remembered names. At least she remembered my name. And I liked it when she would walk by me and whisper, "Vector" and then look the other way and pretend she didn't say anything.

One time she walked by me with her phone to her ear and said, "Is Vector there?"

I said, "Huh?"

And she kept walking and said, "Oh sorry, I am on the phone." I am pretty positive that she wasn't on the phone and was just messing with me. I thought that was pretty cool for a girl.

Chapter 36

Shannon Ungerman came up to my locker on Friday after lunch and put her hand on my elbow. I bet she could feel my heartbeat even from there. I wished I had done some pushups before school. I flexed to try and impress her. I think I did. She asked me about the test. I said I was going to try to get it after school, but I lied. I wasn't going to try and get it after school. I had a meeting after school with the Bully7 in the woods by the soccer goal. The same spot as our first meeting.

The Bully7 met at 3:14pm. I can't tell anyone what was said, but we did talk about what we heard had happened to Josh Crans and Tommy Lunsford. And I did check to make sure that we remembered not to tell anyone if we knew anything. But we didn't know anything because we didn't do anything.

The meeting was very very good. I challenged the guys to remember that we were Better Bullying. And we needed to have a purpose. And the protection money we collected from the **RUNNERS** was going to go to charity. We weren't just changing Range Line. We were changing the whole world.

Chapter 37

Maybe. Maybe not. Maybe. I can't get in trouble because I never admitted we did anything that weekend. Maybe we did and maybe we didn't. Maybe.

Maybe we went to volunteer at the nursing home on Saturday and had pizza with Nate, Joey, and Phoenix again. Maybe we found out who was on the **BILL215** voting committee. And maybe Nate got us a list of the administrators who were voting. And maybe a guy named Mr. Langer was one of them. And maybe we found his house by using Google maps.

And maybe Sunday was a football holiday in that neighborhood. And maybe we went to Mr. Langer's house on Kalt's Lane, which was maybe on the corner by the street. Maybe he had a bunch of people over. And maybe he had satellite tv and the dish was on the street side of his house. And satellite tv's lose their signal if they get bumped or hit with a soccer ball. And maybe we accidentally knocked into his satellite and the tv went blank during the 2nd quarter. And maybe he came outside to ask us to play soccer far away from the house. And maybe he even said please and explained he was having a party and that it was a big game. And maybe one of us said that we were out trying to stay out of trouble because we were under a lot of stress because people were calling us bullies. And maybe Jam said it would be a shame if any of us got expelled because of **BILL215** because we would have so much free time on our hands that we would probably do reckless stuff like running through the neighborhood and punching all the satellites out of anger so we could share our pain with others who were doing nothing wrong. Maybe Dante added, "Hurt people hurt people." And maybe Mr. Langer got scared like a mouse on a glue trap. And maybe someone asked him if it would be unlucky for his satellite to get bumped regularly by a soccer ball during Sunday football. Maybe someone said that we probably wouldn't even play soccer in that neighborhood unless we got expelled.

And maybe Mr. Langer turned white as a white cat. And maybe someone kicked the ball hard against the wall. And maybe Mr. Langer said, "If it was up to me, **BILL215** wouldn't pass." And maybe we said that we wanted to go home and watch football and stay off the streets. Maybe.

Chapter 38

If that story about Mr. Langer was true, and maybe it was not, but if it was true, we knew that we had 1 vote against **BILL215** and needed 1 more. And here is where things get a little wacky. Nate maybe convinced us to try and get another guy on the committee to vote 'yes' for **BILL215**. He promised that if we tried to get a guy named Mr. Hafemeister to vote for **BILL215**, that he would vote against it. Nate said that was just the way Mr. Hafemeister worked. He was positive. He promised that was our only hope. Maybe he told me that.

And so with Nate, Phoenix, and Joey's help, I did the craziest thing ever. I got Serg and we peppered Hafemeister's house with "VOTE **BILL215**" propaganda. It was crazy because if he did vote for it, my Mom would be my gym teacher and my math tutor for a year. I would have rather worn a pink dress to school with bunny slippers than that. But we had to trust those guys. And so we spent an afternoon preparing, and then we spent the late evening attacking. I snuck out of my house and met Serg and Jam. Carl stayed home and prayed for us. And Glenn had no chance to get out because his dad had security cameras and an alarm. And I can't tell you what Mick was doing.

Nate came with us. He was maybe the craziest teenager without a tattoo, piercing, or sword in the universe. We dressed like ninjas and crawled up to Mr. Hafemeister's house through the backyard.

I can't tell you what we did, but we didn't break anything. And we didn't steal anything. And we didn't hurt any pets.

If I told you what we did, we could all get in trouble. Even you maybe. So I won't tell you what happened. But we did use a lot of chalk, peanut butter, and toilet paper. And we did borrow all of his roses from his garden. And we did have "VOTE FOR BILL215" written all over everything possible. Even on the tennis shoes that were left outside. Even on the bird feeder. Or maybe we didn't do any of that.

Chapter 39

Life was happening fast. I was anxious. On Monday my stomach hosted a bonfire. My math test that was going to win me the love of Shannon Ungerman was on Tuesday, the **BILL215** vote was coming up on Thursday, and the Bully7 faced a trial that threatened to destroy us from within.

The Bully7 were so secretive, that I cannot even confirm that we were sworn to secrecy. If we were, we definitely would have promised to never ever never never release the pictures of Tommy Lunsford in his mom's dress and lipstick. That was our leverage to keep him under our thumbs. That was how we got him to stop bad bullying. And it was a code of our honor for one another. It was in the Better Bullying Bylaws. It was a symbol of my leadership. And it was a mess.

Sometime over the weekend, that red lipped awkward photo of Tommy Lunsford in his mother's canary yellow JC Penney dress went viral. It was on Snapchat, Instagram, and posted in a chatroom. The user was NOW.U.C.ME. Of course I didn't care that Tommy was exposed for the freaky dressing muscle child that he was. I cared that one of the Bully7 had broken the rules. They had ignored me. Violated the oath.

NOW.U.C.ME had brought back every insecurity that I had. I felt rejected. I felt betrayed. I felt like giving up on **BILL215** and letting them expel me. The Bully7 were my responsibility, and I felt like I had flopped. I felt like the last kid picked in gym class. I was not who I thought I was. I had failed to keep the order. All was lost. I was as flat as a train track penny.

Chapter 40

One of the things I learned from a guy who told me never to tell anyone what I learned from him, was that if I ever felt nervous, I should fake positive. He told me to pretend to be an actor in my own movie. And that was what I did when I called the Bully7 together for a 3:14pm emergency meeting in the woods by the soccer goal.

I knew one of them had betrayed me. Maybe it was Dante. I knew one of them had tested me. Maybe it was Serg. I knew I had been undermined. Maybe it was Glenn. I just didn't know what to do about it. Maybe it was Carl. I wanted to cry. Maybe it was Mick. I didn't cry. I would never let them see me cry. Especially since one of them was 'NOW.U.C.ME.'

I couldn't look them in the eyes so I stared at my shoes. To keep from quivering, I shifted my jaw like hips around a hoola hoop, "This is our first great test. There has been a fracture in our force."

I didn't even have to mention the photos. Everyone knew what I was talking about. One of us was guilty. We all looked at each other like when you smell dog poop and look around at shoes to see who stepped in it.

Serg spoke first. 2 words as always, "Wasn't me."

Jam, "This is unhealthy. We made a promise. Who did it? I didn't."

Glenn quoted another old dead guy, "It is more shameful to distrust our friends than to be deceived by them." And he closed his eyes.

Dante, "Don't look at me. This is bad bullying. I didn't sign up for this."

Mick, "This is just unjust." And he looked at Carl.

Carl, "With God as my witness it wasn't me."

Our body language was terrible. Guys were sagging their shoulders like crust on wet bread. I was the only one who hadn't said anything. I thought about lying to say I had done it just to keep the group together. To keep spirits up. But I hadn't done it.

These guys were my brothers. Committed to Better Bullying. They had been a part of the best weeks of my life. I refused to believe anything bad about them.

I faked confidence and said, "I believe each of you. I hope you believe me. I trust you. Something is wrong here, and it is not us. Let's move forward."

Chapter 41

My feet were getting wet, but I didn't care. We couldn't end on a low. We each shared a bullying highlight from the week.

Carl said he put Joel Shanker in a headlock until he confessed his sins and prayed for forgiveness.

Jam caught Steven Mills smoking out back and made him eat his last 2 cigarettes.

Serg pulled out a French film that he had snatched from an artistic **RUNNER** named Drewsy and said, "USA ONLY!!!" And then he snapped the DVD in half.

Glenn continued to drop deepness, "Kites rise highest against the wind, not with it." He explained, "I broke Joey Joyce's calculator and forced him to memorize his times tables."

Dante, "Hans Schmidt just bought a pair of sneakers for $170. I made him give $20 towards clean water in Africa or his shoes were gonna end up in dirty water at Range Line."

Mick, "Ryan Melon Morris was making fun of Mr. Patel's turban. He won't be making fun of anything until he gets those 8 stitches out of his lip."

Me, "I saw that **RUNNER** John Denler throw a rock at a homeless guy. Serg and I followed him and saw him go into a porta-potty. We tipped it over with John inside it."

Better Bullying was forcing **RUNNERS** to change for their own good. I was wildly proud of each success story. But I couldn't help wondering who the phony was among us. I had to figure out who had posted the photos of Tommy Lunsford in his mom's canary yellow dress.

Chapter 42

On Tuesday we pretended like everything was normal at school, but things were far from perfect. We still didn't know how the Tommy Lunsford photos had escaped from our secret circle. And we knew that the rest of our lives might be decided 2 days later in a decision on **BILL215**. And we had actually harassed one of the voters to cast a YES. And I had a test that Shannon Ungerman was purring at me about. She wanted me to steal the master copy, but I didn't steal it. I did something even crazier. I studied.

Shannon Ungerman was warm on me about math. Like pee in a pool. I didn't want to let her down, but I also didn't want to cheat. I was leading Better Bullying, and I felt like it would distract from our cause if I got caught. So I studied like a scientist.

And then I told Shannon to sit next to me. I told her that I had seen the answer sheet and memorized it, but couldn't steal it because the security guard was walking the halls. I said I knew most of the answers and I promised to write them as big as John Hancock. John Hancock wrote big when he signed the Declaration of Independence. We learned that in History. A bunch of awesome old rich white guys signed it too, but none as big as John Hancock. John Hancock might not have been proud of me for helping someone cheat, but I think he would have wanted me to have a girlfriend. He fought for that freedom and signed big for it.

We had a seating chart in Mr. Blade's class, and Shannon didn't sit next to me, but she was a clever girl. Before the test she told Mr. Blade that chunky Rudy Will kept looking at her toes. Mr. Blade said that didn't make sense because she had shoes and socks on. Shannon said he could trust her that she had toes. And that she would think it was creepy if she had to prove it to him by showing him. And she didn't want to get her lawyer involved and asked that she be moved to another chair. The only open seat was the one next to me. She moved there on her own. And then Mr. Blade handed out the test.

John Hancock would have been proud as I wrote as big as a flag and we both got A's. And Shannon Ungerman gave me a huge hug and kissed my cheek. It was glorious. I felt like someone had plugged me in. I was alive.

Chapter 43

My excitement from the kiss couldn't stop the gnawing in my head. I couldn't stop wondering who rejected my leadership. I hated being rejected. It made me feel unimportant. Insignificant. Unpopular. Fatherless. Low. I tried to fake confidence that it didn't matter, but it did matter. You can't fake confidence within yourself.

I needed to know if one of the Bully7 had betrayed me. I thought that maybe one of them didn't agree with the bylaws. Maybe one of them wanted to steal Shannon Ungerman from me. Maybe one wanted to be the real leader. Maybe they were meeting behind my back. I was sliced with uncertainty. What had been the best week of my life seemed at that moment to be the worst.

I didn't care that people were talking about Tommy Lunsford behind his back. Or that someone wrote "TAMMY LUNSFORD" on his locker in lipstick. He was a bad bully. He could defend himself. We didn't have him under control anymore, but I had bigger problems. I had to know who had posted the photos of him. I had to know who used the username 'NOW.U.C.ME' and how to handle him.

Nate from the nursing home gave me some advice, and I spent Tuesday night on the hunt. I Googled 'NOW.U.C.ME' and found 5,700 results in .40 seconds. There were a lot of things that came up under "NOW.U.C.ME", but none of them were tied to our case. I needed something more. And it took time. Tons of searches. After many

many silly peek-a-boo videos, I found the leprechaun's pot of gold. The end of the rainbow for me was a site called YouTube. You might have heard of it. They post videos and people leave comments. And a lot of times people keep a username from other sites. And when I found 'NOW.U.C.ME.', I knew that I just had to follow the bread crumb trail.

Chapter 44

I was really hoping it wasn't Jam who had betrayed me. He was my best friend. In my armpits I knew it wasn't him, but I couldn't be sure of anything. I couldn't trust anyone. Even at school that day, I felt like people were talking about me. And that night when I got a scam email telling me that I had inherited money from Nigeria, I wondered if it might be 'NOW.U.C.ME.' messing with me. I was paranoid. I had to know. So I started to study for clues from anyone who had 'liked' the Instagram photos of Tommy Lunsford.

Right as I started to search the web, Timmy came in and asked me what I was doing. I wasn't mad at him, I was mad at the world. But I pushed the bullying limits. I felt like a gorilla. I grabbed and twisted him. I squeezed and shook him. I screamed and smashed. My knuckles joined his ribs and my foot volleyed his butt. He cried. My mom yelled. I lied.

And it didn't make me feel any better. I told him to shut his pie hole and to tell her we were wrestling and he hurt his hand slapping me. It worked, but like I said, I didn't feel any better.

And then I went back to the computer and I went through all of the YouTube favorites like nothing happened. I hunted. I sniffed out every possibility. I read all of the comments. I wondered if Mick might have caved. Or if Carl had felt God telling him to do it. I didn't know, but I was getting closer to figuring it out as I read more and more comments. And then the case broke. A hint. A clue. A photo. A name. And I couldn't believe what had happened.

'NOW.U.C.ME.' had been tagged in a video. It was a family on vacation on the beach. It was a few years ago. It was sunny and windy. It was a little bit blurry. It was Josh Crans.

Chapter 45

I was so unhappy. I clenched my fists and wanted to hurt someone. I called for my little brother. I never wanted him to feel the misery that I drowning in. I wanted to toughen him up as much as possible so that he was ready for the 7th grade. His name exploded from my rage, "TIMMMMYY!!!!"

I knew I should have been pounding the pulp out of Josh Crans instead of Timmy, but Timmy was a lot closer. Timmy had to have heard me, but he didn't obey my call for him. I yelled again and this time I added, "NOWWWWWWW." Timmy didn't come. He was hiding.

I began to craze. I kept telling myself it was for Timmy's own good, but something seemed wrong that night. It didn't seem good.

And I realized it had been a while since I gave him a licking. Before that night, I hadn't been bullying him much at all since I had been getting popular and helping Shannon fall in love with me. It was weird. Odd. And in that moment I felt a little sick about it. But none of that mattered. Josh Crans was what mattered. And I decided to leave Timmy in his hiding spot.

Instead, I called for an emergency phone meeting with the Bully7. We used an encrypted line and spoke in code. I told them that I knew who had released the Tommy Lunsford photos and I could guess why. After we had attacked Josh Crans in the bathroom and given him the swirly, purple nurple, wedgie combo, he became aware that he was powerless against our united strength. He knew that he couldn't join us, so he tried to destroy us.

Tommy Lunsford must have told him about how his account had been hacked and someone got his pictures. And how someone had sworn to secrecy if he would stop bad bullying. Josh must have figured out that it was us. And that if he could turn us against each other, they could turn back to their bullying ways.

It was an incredible twist of events on that Tuesday. I was restored in my control. I was relevant. I was popular again. It was one of the greatest days of my life. And we decided that Wednesday would be the worst day of Josh Crans's life.

It had been a stressful few days of suspicion. It was about to be a wonderful morning of revenge.

Chapter 46

Josh Crans needs a new padlock. During 2nd hour gym class, a few of us might have gone into the bathroom and wrenched his locker open. We might have put peanut butter in the pockets of his jeans. We might have cut the toes out of his socks. We might have put a mysteriously stained pair of underwear in his favorite hat. We might have rubbed smelly Limburger cheese in the armpits of his shirt. We might have cut the shoelaces out of his sneakers. We might have spray painted his shoes pink. We might have put his belt in the urinal. We might have pulled the drawstring out of his hoody, irretrievably halfway. We might have changed all of the contacts in his phone to 'HONEY BOO BOO'. We might have sent his Aunt Mary a very mean text message from his phone that said, "I can smell your toes in Texas." We might have texted Principal Deitz from his phone saying, "Snitches get stitches." We might have glued the zipper of his pants halfway down. We might have cut the bottom out of his backpack. We might have turned the language on his laptop screen to Japanese. We might have deleted all of his apps. We might have put itching powder into the butt of his boxers.

We might have done all of those things. I can't say if we did or didn't. I can tell you that Josh Crans limped around the rest of the day scratching his butt. Smelling like cheese. With his pants sagging. And his fly half down. And he refused to have the peanut butter and jelly sandwiches for lunch.

Chapter 47

Thursday was an amazing and horrible day. Truly memorable. Totally unpredictable. Wow. Whoa. Dang.

Shannon Ungerman came to my locker again and put her hand on my shoulder. It felt like she was announcing I was King of the World. A knight. She didn't say I was her boyfriend. What she said was, "Can we sit next to each other in History class too?"

My words jumped out of my face, "Yes yes yes."

And she whispered warm air in my ear, "Good because we have a quiz next week."

I got goosebumps. School was bringing us together. Studying really did make a difference. It made me go from single to having a girlfriend. Probably. We weren't official yet, but probably.

And there was no doubt I was popular. People knew me. They knew the Bully7. Everyone was talking about Josh Crans and what had happened to him. They were talking about him and smelling him. And more and more kids wanted to sign up for

our protection program. More and more kids
wanted to be safe and follow Better Bullying.
        Everything was great. Amazing.
Really really great. A dream without drool
on the pillow. Popular at last. The only
problem was that if **BILL215** was passed
that night, it was all going to end.

Chapter 48

        I could write a book about that
Thursday. We were the buzz. The Bully7
were it. And people were talking about me.
A group of star athletes in the hallway
called me over. That was the group of
friends I wanted to be in before the Bully7.
They were the coolest kids on this side of
the Mason-Dixon line. (We just learned
about that in History. I was listening so I
could help Shannon on the next test.)
        It was Cam Hoffman, Griffin and
Brayden Engroff, Sela Lynk, Miles Engstrom,
Holden Heckenberger, Madison Williams,
Nora Seren, and Tyson Dusosky. Those kids
always smelled good, won the gym class relay
races, and had shoes that matched their
shirts.
        Tyson and Cam were going to be
professional hockey somethings someday
somewhere. Tyson said he saw me talking to

Shannon Ungerman and asked if we were friends. I confirmed. Cam said, "I love it. From zero to hero in a day." I couldn't believe he knew my name. They had a best friend named Noah Moses Cohen, and the 3 of them were so popular they didn't even know they were popular. And they knew my name. It really happened. I was sort of popular. And I knew it.

But being known isn't always a good thing. And Mr. Blade reminded me of that in math class. He called me up to the front of the room and asked me to read the announcements for the day. He had never done that before, but I soon knew why he did that day.

I read it, "Tomorrow for lunch we will have tater tots and hamburgers. Basketball tryouts will start next month. You need to have a physical completed to participate. And there is an open forum tonight in the assembly hall on **BILL215**." I started to stutter. Kids gulped. I think that they started laughing at me. They knew that I knew that they knew that I knew that **BILL215** was about me and the whole Bully7. "Billtaaa.... Billta.....Billta." I couldn't get the words out. I stammered more. I couldn't believe what he had me reading, my words chugged, "Bababababa." And then something just clicked. I remembered to fake confidence, "Bababa **BILL215** is part of Principal Deitz's push to make Range Line Elementary School a safer place. **BILL215** would allow Principal Deitz to expel bullies and force them into home schooling." It was crazy. It was like I was reading my own obituary. I so badly wanted to be funny, but it was so bizarre. And then I just decided to go for it. I added my own announcement, "You should come to support this new trend called Better Bullying. Mr. Blade is going to be there in a cheerleader's skirt, with a cat on a leash, wearing his lovely cologne that smells like a new shoe. And he is going to turtle wax his bald head before he leaves the house. It's going to be so shiny that aliens will see it from their planet." And then I looked at Mr. Blade and said, "Should I just go the Principal's Office now?" and I walked out the door.

Chapter 49

I didn't care. I cared, but I didn't care. Mr. Blade was a bully. He was picking on me in front of the class. He was trying to use me to make himself feel better. He was probably trying to right some wrong in his life by abusing me. He probably didn't even

74

realize that I was a symbol of the part of himself that he hated. Hurt people, hurt people. There was likely some lack of control that he had experienced in his life that was causing him to try and gain control over other situations. His weakness became his strength. He was a bully without direction. Self serving. A bad bully.

Chapter 50

I sat in the office waiting for Mr. Deitz when Mr. Sean Peterson wheeled by. Mr. Sean wasn't on a bike or anything. He was in a wheelchair. If you were brave and asked him what happened, he would say he was faking the handicap for the good parking spots. Or he would tell some story about how he donated his legs to a swimsuit model who is now rich and famous.

I heard the true story was that before Mr. Sean was our Assistant Principal, he was an adventure seeker. He didn't use drugs, but used life to get high. He loved to hitchhike and was always looking for a new experience. And one time he chased a feeling and fell. He slipped from a big pole and landed on the ground and couldn't get back up.

I really liked Mr. Sean. He had racing stripes on his wheelchair and a different bumper sticker on the back every week. One week it said, "What if all the children in the whole world farted at once?" And another time it said, "Watch out for the crazy kid behind me." And when he wheeled by me that day it said, "This is how I roll."

Mr. Sean talked to me like he always did. He talked to me like he was once a kid who made mistakes. And he listened. And when he said something, he was speaking to me and not at me. There is a difference.

Chapter 51

Mr. Sean asked me about the Bully7 and I listed the amazing things we were accomplishing at Range Line. **RUNNERS** were doing their homework, eating less sugar, turning back to God, and looking at the global water issue.

He asked about the difference between Better Bullying and regular bullying. I told him that it wasn't bullying if we were forcing them to do what was good for them. It was kind of tough love.

His face scrunched like he was trying to touch his nose to his forehead. He was thinking.

And then I told him about what had happened in Mr. Blade's class. I told him Mr. Blade didn't like me any more. And how he used to really like me, but things changed when he got his Jeep.

Mr. Sean asked what had happened. "What had happened was, that Mr. Blade was one of my favorites. He was cool. Until he showed a picture of his new jeep to the class and I asked how much it cost and if I could have a ride in it. Mr. Blade got annoyed and embarrassed me. He said, **'I'm not a taxi service. If you want a ride you need to pay for it.'**"

Kim McMullen, a stunning blonde girl who was as popular as ice cream said, "Burn!" and licked her finger and made a sizzling sound. I was humiliated. I was red-faced. I didn't like getting laughed at. And then I said, "Well if I paid you, then you would be a taxi service." Nora Seren laughed so hard she farted. And Birdie Lasusa smelled it and made a gagging noise like she was at the dentist. And then Mr. Blade was red-faced. Burn back.

Chapter 52

I also told Mr. Sean about **BILL215**, my momma, Kelly, the nursing home, Shannon Ungerman, and I told him about Timmy. I told him I was just starting to get popular. And that I was just about to have my first girlfriend. And I told him a lot about my friend Kelly. I told him about how she was always making me laugh. And how she was skinny, but not like a deer. And how she passed me notes in class that said things like, "Remember when we went to mall and got ice cream and, oh no, that hasn't happened yet."

And I told him about how cute Shannon Ungerman was in polka dots. And how she was kind of mean to people who weren't popular. And how her friends rated other girls by looks on a scale of 1-11. And they posted those rankings on their blog. And that her friends teased girls that didn't have nice ears. And she one time said that Lori had a nose so big she could breathe under water. And another time she made Sybil cry when she asked if she ever thanked the dead woman who donated the wig she was wearing. I didn't like that stuff about her, but I was pretty sure she would change if we were dating.

Mr. Sean laughed through his teeth when I said that and I asked why. He didn't answer but asked me a question back, "Why do you think she will stop being mean if you guys are dating?"

I told him about how once I started to get popular, I stopped bullying Timmy mostly. And the closer I got to having a girlfriend, the less I wanted to fix him. And the less I hurt him. And how when I got mad that night before, that I wanted to make like Little Bunny Foo Foo, and hop through the forest of his room, and pick him up like ground mice, and bop him on the head.

Mr. Sean let me talk a lot. He let me say that I thought I could date Shannon Ungerman and make her happy. And if she was happy, she would change and be nice.

Mr. Sean just listened. I was supposed to go into Mr. Deitz's office, but he told the grumpy secretary in the brown sweater with shoulder pads that he was taking care of it. He was taking care of me. He asked if I thought there was any connection with me being happy and how often I bullied my brother.

I said that I bullied Timmy less when I was popular. Less when I had a girl that liked me. Less when I was King of Better Bullying. Less when I had great and strong

friends. Less when I wasn't getting bullied.
Basically, I bullied less when I was happy.

Chapter 53

Mr. Sean was careful with his words
like they were made of glass. He gently
said, "If you believe in Better Bullying, why
do you only do it when you are mad or sad?"

It was like he had stolen my brain and
fixed it. He unlocked something. I hadn't
ever realized it. I was bullying others
because I got bullied.

Other kids and girls and Mr. Blade.
They had all bullied me. And they made me
feel weak. And unimportant. And I guess I
had to realize that I was bullying because I
was bullied. I asked him how he was always
so happy.

He looked me in the pupil and said, "I
do 3 things. I hug my mom every time I see
her. I choose to find the best in every
person. And I see life as an adventure."

He handed me a short poem he had
written and that he read every time he was
upset. It said,

"There is a part of me
That always knows how
To feel wonderful"

It didn't rhyme, but it was a great poem for me. Bullying Timmy didn't make me feel wonderful. Good people and doing good things did.

I never saw Mr. Deitz that morning. I didn't need to. I saw someone much more powerful and important that day. I saw myself.

The world looked different when I walked back to class. I realized a lot about my life. And I realized something about Mr. Sean. Mr. Sean fell off a pole and would never be able to stand up again. But that fall could never keep him down.

Chapter 54

I was numb for the rest of the day. Like when I went to the dentist and would lick the spot where the doctor injected me before harvesting my face for cavities. And that day was a little like that. I just couldn't feel anything. And I kept wondering when I would snap back.

I didn't wake up when I walked into Mr. Blade's class and he said, "Hector Vector is back. Maybe Principal Deitz taught him to hold a pencil. Or fixed his chipped tooth with some white bubble gum."

I just sat down and said, "Hurt people hurt people."

I couldn't hear if people laughed. Mr. Blade said something. I can't remember. He said something again and I just repeated myself. "Hurt people hurt people."

Someone told me later that he yelled. I didn't hear it. I didn't feel it. I was going through my book bag looking for a sharp pencil. I never had a sharp pencil.

Later I would find out that Kelly raised her hand and said, "I think he is talking about himself and not you." She was trying to get me out of more trouble.

And Shannon Ungerman said, "Or he is talking about Kelly sitting on someone's lap. Heavy people hurt people."

I didn't hear it. I didn't hear anything. I was just thinking about how that could be my last class. And I daydreamed about Better Bullying. And wondered if my mom was going to make me do sit-ups in home school gym class if **BILL215** passed that night. I hate sit-ups.

Chapter 55

The assembly hall for the **BILL215** meeting was as bright as the moon and smelled like sweaty sun hair. And it was as crowded as a crowded elevator.

There were a bunch of starchy adults in attendance and some local press. And a lot of students that were accused of bullying. That included the Bully7, Tommy Lunsford, Josh Crans, and even Shannon Ungerman and a few of her friends. I guess that their blog had come to the attention of the school and it was considered cyber bullying.

There was a raised table with some microphones for the panel of 3, and a microphone on the floor level for questions. The panel of 3 was our Principal Mr. Deitz, Mr. Langer (who had the satellite tv dish), and Mr. Hafemeister (whose house we attacked). After the presentation and comments from the audience, the 3 were to vote publicly on **BILL215**. They would be voting on my life.

There was a lot that happened, but the only important thing to tell is that a guy in suspenders and a fish tie read a legal sounding document. And then he opened it up for public comments. He asked people to stand up if they wanted to speak in favor of **BILL215**. I couldn't believe what happened next. It was like a church service.

Chapter 56

It was like a church service because everyone stood up at once. There was a Walmart length line to speak against the bullies at Range Line Elementary. It was a snaking reminder of how my life was over. And how my mom was going to be my new History teacher. And English. And Spanish. And everything. I had no chance. I was headed to home schooling. I was never going to have a girlfriend. I was going to die alone. I was positive.

Speaker after speaker stepped to the microphone and pierced eardrums with stories of how their child had been bullied. Harassed. Tormented. Thugged. Oppressed. Persecuted. Tyrannized. Robbed. Intimidated.

Not one person thanked us. Not one parent appreciated that we were partnering with them through Better Bullying. It was just negative air. I felt used. It was as if they were unable to see healing under the bandages. It was as if they had forgotten that whatever doesn't kill you makes you stronger. It was as if they didn't believe in Better Bullying.

Chapter 57

The Bully7 had helped kids toughen up, get in shape, grow spiritually, dress better, become more American, and to see clearer on racial issues. We had successfully forced children into becoming better people. And we protected them from bad bullies. All we demanded was that they make a tax deductible donation so African kids wouldn't have to drink puddle water. That was all we demanded. And all we got back was heat.

They called us thugs. They said we were the Junior Mafia. Like a gang of villains. Rogues. Goons.

It was like I kicked a beehive. There was a swarm of them. And their words stung.

Their perspective was warped. Emotions were bubbling. And **BILL215** looked like a done deal.

Chapter 58

Once it stopped raining hatred, a lawyer for Josh Crans's family stood up and stated that he would file an injunction if Josh was expelled. He said that it was too much unilateral power for a Principal to have. He used a bunch of fancy words.

The guy in suspenders thanked him, and reminded him that **BILL215** getting passed only gave a Principal permission to expel, but did not mean that he would. And he believed that Josh was safe. He assured the lawyer that the staff knew Josh Crans was a wonderful kid. I laughed out of my nose at that nonsense. I knew who Josh Crans really was. He was a bad bully, but that didn't matter.

After the lawyer, no one else spoke. It was like a concert of crickets. No one dropped a pin. I'm sure of it.

The accused bullies were not allowed to say anything. They believed giving bullies a microphone was the power we wanted. And they didn't trust us. They said that if no other students would defend us, then we shouldn't be able to defend ourselves.

Things weren't looking good. There was still hope that **BILL215** would fail on the vote. We needed Mr. Langer to remember his fragile satellite tv. And we needed nursing home Nate's guess about Mr. Hafemeister to be right.

And then a terrible thing happened. It was a deadly twist. Mr. Langer announced that he was retiring, and that he wouldn't be able to cast a vote. And he wanted to be there to congratulate his replacement on the board. His replacement would cast the vote and serve on the committee.

My back ached. My stomach knotted. My throat lumped. My eyes watered.

Mr. Langer was our winning vote. We knew Mr. Deitz would vote for **BILL215**. We hoped Mr. Hafemeister would vote against it. Mr. Langer was our only hope. It was bad. And then it got worse. Much worse.

I couldn't believe it when I heard it. And then I couldn't believe it when I saw it. Mr. Langer said, "I would like to thank you all and introduce my replacement. Mister Blade."

If I hadn't seen that bald head shine with my own eyes I wouldn't have believed. Mr. Blade stood up, walked to the podium, and shook hands. All I could do was shake my head. We were cooked.

Chapter 59

We needed 2 of 3 votes to win, and Mr. Langer was our only guarantee. That meant even with Mr. Hafemeister, we only had 1 on our side. And we had vandalized his house with "VOTE FOR **BILL215**." And sure as sugar is sweet, Mr. Blade was going to vote against us. We might lose 0-3!!!

I was trying to make myself feel better. Maybe my mom would let me sleep in since 1st hour would be at the kitchen table. Maybe I would get desserts with home schooled lunch. Maybe I wouldn't have to ever shower because I wouldn't leave the house. None of these things made me feel better. I wanted to be at Range Line. I wanted to be popular for more than a week. I wanted a girlfriend.

And I just wanted the vote to be over. And it almost was. The guy in the suspenders asked if there was anyone who wanted to speak against **BILL215**. Mr. Blade wasn't supposed to say anything, but he did. He blabbed, "I am excited to be a part of the committee and the excellence at Range Line Elementary. We have a bullying problem, and I am hoping we can clean house. We even have one young man who thinks bullying is okay. He looks past his own chipped tooth and bony elbows. He forgets that he holds a pencil like it is a flute and tries to bully others who aren't perfect. His group of friends have formed a club. They are **homeboys**. Pretty soon, they will be **home schooled.**

He was talking about me. He was talking about the Bully7. Josh Crans couldn't break us apart. Tommy Lunsford couldn't bring us down. But it was over. We were going to lose that vote. I knew it.

The guy in the suspenders thanked Mr. Blade and gave him a bro hug. And then said, "At this time, we will turn off the microphones, and turn to the vote for **BILL215**."

It was all over. And then a voice from the crowd yelled, "WAIT!!!!!"

Chapter 60

If a voice could be made of delicious chocolate milk, it would have sounded like the one that yelped from the crowd. It was familiar. It was Kelly.

Kelly walked to the microphone like she was trying to win a race. And maybe she was. Only I didn't know whose team she was on.

We had become friends. I *liked* her. Not *like like*. Well, maybe a little *like like*. But she had been called an ugly cow dog by Josh Crans. And just that day Shannon Ungerman had said she would hurt a trampoline if she jumped on it. I didn't understand why people joked about her weight, but they did. She wasn't skinny as a deer, but I didn't care. Why would anyone care?

I didn't know if Kelly was with us or against us, "I have been a victim of bullying at Range Line. I have been called a farm of names. Cow, pig, dog, and even an aardvark. I didn't even know what that was.

"I have cried. And cried. And cried. No bully has ever punched me or kicked me or pushed me. But I have been hurt. I have been really really hurt.

"Some people believe that there can be Better Bullying. I don't think so. But I think that bullies can get better.

"Mr. Blade just bullied a student with his anonymous remarks about a chipped tooth and a weird way to hold a pencil. Are we going to expel him?

"And what about when all of the bullies are gone? What happens to them? How is this decided? Isn't one person having power over another how bullying works?

"A bully once made me feel very pretty after another bully made me feel really ugly. He told me I wasn't skinny like a deer but that I was pretty great. And he explained the other bully to me. He told me that hurt people hurt people.

"And hurt people do hurt people. And I think that is what we are doing if we allow them to be expelled."

Chapter 61

Her speech was slow-clap good. Amazing. It was as amazing as the Pythagorean Theorem that I learned about in Geometry when I studied so I wouldn't have to cheat to get Shannon Ungerman to be my girlfriend when I let her cheat.

Kelly was really really great. I thought I loved her for a minute. And then I remembered I was about to be expelled and it was no time for love.

Mr. Blade voted first. He said, "Thank you for that sophMORONIC....I mean sophomoric speech. I vote YES for **BILL215**."

He made an adult joke. I didn't get it. I heard the word moronic I think. It would probably have been moronic to tell someone I didn't get it. It didn't matter. We were down 1 to 0. There was 1 vote to pass **BILL215** and no votes against it.

Then it was Mr. Hafemeister's turn. He said, "I have been a victim of bullying myself. Someone has tried to get me to vote for **BILL215**. I cannot. I will not. I do not. I vote against **BILL215**. Please leave my car and flowers alone whoever you are."

Nursing home Nate was a genius. It was 1 to 1. One vote to pass **BILL215**. One vote to reject **BILL215**. If Mr. Langer was there, it would have been a big win for us. But Mr. Langer wasn't there. It was Mr. Deitz. He was the one that wanted a bully free school. He was the one that could give himself the power. He was the tiebreaker. He was my life breaker.

Chapter 62

And then I heard an amazing noise. I heard a rip. It sounded like Velcro. I was confused when I looked up to see Mr. Deitz with 2 torn pieces of paper in his hand. I didn't know what had happened. Well, what had happened was, Mr. Deitz ripped up **BILL215**. He voted against it. By tearing that piece of paper in half, he taped my life back together. We won 2-1. There were 2 votes against **BILL215** and only 1 in favor. Kelly had persuaded him. She was a superhero.

Mr. Deitz was talking to all of us but he was looking right at me. He said, "Today I am voting against myself. I am voting for you. You are my students. Even the bullies. I am trusting that our school will be better with you than without you. I am trusting you to see that there isn't Better Bullying, but better ways to help your classmates. I am trusting that even though hurt people hurt people, that things can change. Hurt people can help people.

"I have changed a lot of things since I became principal here, and I am not done yet."

Max Perkins yelled, "BRING BACK DODGEBALL!!!!!"

Mr. Deitz pointed in the direction it came from but looked the other way and said, "I am ignoring you on purpose."

Everyone laughed. Everyone except Mr. Blade. Mr. Blade was so red he was almost purple. The vein in his forehead was swollen and twitching. He was mad, but I didn't care. I would have to deal with him another day. I was just grateful there would be another day. I was not getting expelled into home schooling.

Chapter 63

Some things changed around Range Line Elementary after **BILL215** was shredded. I know I did. And some things stayed the same. I know Mr. Blade did. That is another story for another time, especially the part about the prank with his online dating friend and the frogs.

After the vote, Mr. Sean started to meet with the BULLY7 to help us to use our passions for good things. We even renamed our group. He taught us how to make a good difference without karate chopping kids in the throat and taking their money. And he helped us to understand what made us so passionate.

Jam's dad taught him the value of sports and hard work, and he wants other kids to know it too. He loves his dad. His heart is right.

Carl wants kids to go to Heaven. He thinks they need to go to church first. His heart is right.

Dante wants people to know that we have water in our toilets cleaner than many people in the world drink. He hopes we spend less on shoes and diamonds and more to help the poor. His heart is right.

Serg knows we live in a great country. And that we take it for granted. And he wants others to appreciate our freedom and how great it is to be an American. His heart is right.

Glenn knows the road to success is often through education. And that he will pay more taxes if others can't. His heart is right.

Mick knows that racial hatred often starts as a small seed and grows into a nasty thorn bush. He wants kids to look past skin color. His heart is right.

And I just want kids to get tougher. I want Timmy to get tougher in case his dad leaves like mine did. I don't want children to suffer like me. I want them to be numb so that they can survive this bitter world. My heart is right.

Chapter 64

I tried to tell Mr. Sean that we were better bullies because what we did was for the **RUNNER'S** good. And we proved it. We had results. Glenn made a chart.

And I told him that Better Bullying was what real life people did in real life. Adults on Facebook made other adults feel guilty about their opinions. And you can get shamed for being different. And you can be scared into being religious. And there is pressure to give away money.

My Sean just looked at me and, "Well, maybe adults can be bad bullies too."

Wow. Mr. Sean showed me that even though my heart was right, my actions weren't. And he didn't teach me this by bullying me or expelling me or yelling at me or embarrassing me. He showed me by making me think. And by caring about me. And by talking to me like he was once a kid who made a lot of mistakes, even when his heart was right.

Chapter 65

I am not perfect yet. I am getting better. I know one thing for sure, and that is that I don't know much of anything. I'm only 12. I still have time.

I'm not really popular anymore. And once I stopped letting Shannon Ungerman sit next to me, I think she stopped loving me. I don't miss her at all. Well, maybe I miss the idea of being her boyfriend and what people would say. We had a good thing, but she wasn't really a good thing. She is kind of mean. She still wants to be a bully. And I just want to be happy and help people.

Maybe some day, I will cut toenails at the nursing home. And we are still raising money to build a well for clean water in Africa. I am asking kids to drink tap water instead of buying soda, and to donate the money they save. We have a ways to go. And I heard that Dante just made JC Cruz drink out of a playground puddle because he refused to donate. I guess we have a long long way to go.

I don't compare Better Bullying to bad bullying much anymore. It's like saying one Brussels sprout tastes better than another. Really, both taste terrible, even if one is mushy and worse. Better Bullying is healthier than bad bullying, but both are bad.

I can't force someone to change, but if I treat them like Mr. Sean treats me, then they might improve like I did. And I know now that if I only bully Timmy when I am upset or annoyed, then I probably shouldn't do it. Hurt people hurting people. That's probably not a good idea.

Chapter 66

Things have gotten better. I accidentally got good grades because I started studying. I stopped sulking about my dad and started appreciating my Mom. I hug her every morning. And I haven't punched Timmy in 16 days. That's a record. And I maybe even took him to the nursing home to destroy some immodest trash talking bully Grandma who was undefeated at Connect4.

I didn't become Saint Vector or anything. Especially after what happened in the parking lot with Mr. Blade and his Jeep. And something had to be done about the angry 6th grade mom militia. And that one time I was just protecting Timmy's best friend Reis Von Ruden.

And I did owe Joey and Nate a favor. That night got out of control. Or maybe it didn't. I am not allowed to say.

And I still think some cupcake kids need to toughen up, especially Timmy. But I am not going to put his head in the toilet for a while. Not at school at least.

I am done with bullying at Range Line. Almost. Nearly. Practically. I still have weak moments of the flesh where I make mistakes. Some big mistakes. Or maybe I don't. I can't say.

Maybe I signed Josh Crans up as an 18 year old for the Army. And maybe they keep calling his house and knocking on his door. And maybe I anonymously ordered the world's largest collection of used bubble gum on freecycle.com and had it delivered to him and called the news and they wrote an article. Maybe I didn't.

And though I do my best to not talk back to Mr. Blade, maybe I found his phone number in a school district directory and put an advertisement in the paper for "FREE GUITARS" and listed his number. And maybe he gets hundreds of calls a day. And maybe I did have some turtle wax shipped to his house. And maybe I accidentally wrote an amazing letter on his behalf and accidentally wrote his name as 'Mrs. Blade' and he won a teaching award from the magazine, "Women's Monthly."

Chapter 67

I am not a bully, but I am not going to win any student of the year awards. Not this year. I am just grateful to be a student still. And I thanked Mr. Deitz for giving me another chance. And he said he believed in me. And those words were like a trophy.

And I think I might like Kelly Chrisinger. And I might *like like* her too. She sent me a text today and said, "i lost my phone. can u call it plz?" And I did and she answered and said, "Found it." And we talked for an hour. She didn't lose it. She tricked me. That's pretty funny.

And she kept me out of home schooling. She saved my life I think. She saved all of us. Even Josh Crans and Shannon Ungerman. After all that they did and said to her, she still didn't want bad

things to happen to them. That's a great
girl. She treats other people like she wants
to be treated. That's the kind of girl I want
to have as my friend. And as my first
girlfriend I hope. She taught me something
important. I guess it's true. Hurt people
can help people.

The End....for now